The Dinosaur
Next Door

Crabtree Publishing Company
www.crabtreebooks.com
1-800-387-7650

PMB 16A, 350 Fifth Ave.   616 Welland Ave.
Suite 3308,   St. Catharines, ON
New York, NY   L2M 5V6

Published by Crabtree Publishing in 2010

Series Editor: Jackie Hamley
Editors: Melanie Palmer, Reagan Miller
Series Advisor: Dr. Hilary Minns
Series Designer: Peter Scoulding
Editorial Director: Kathy Middleton

Text © Joan Stimson 2008
Illustration © Andy Elkerton 2008

The rights of the author and the illustrator
of this Work have been asserted.

First published in 2008
by Franklin Watts
(A division of Hachette
Children's Books)

Library and Archives Canada
Cataloguing in Publication

Stimson, Joan
  The dinosaur next door / Joan Stimson ;
illustrated by Andy Elkerton.

(Tadpoles)
ISBN 978-0-7787-3873-2 (bound).--
ISBN 978-0-7787-3904-3 (pbk.)

    1. Readers (Primary). 2. Readers--Dinosaurs.
I. Alkerton, Andy II. Title. III. Series: Tadpoles
(St. Catharines, Ont.)

PE1117.T33 2009g   428.6   C2009-903991-5

Library of Congress
Cataloging-in-Publication Data

Stimson, Joan.
  The dinosaur next door / by Joan Stimson ;
illustrated by Andy Elkerton.
      p. cm. -- (Tadpoles)
  Summary: Tom discovers a red and purple
dinosaur in his neighbor's yard one night.
  ISBN 978-0-7787-3904-3 (pbk.) -- ISBN
978-0-7787-3873-2 (reinforced library binding)
  [1. Dinosaurs--Fiction.] I. Elkerton, Andy, ill.
II. Title. III. Series.

  PZ7.S86015Din 2010
  [E]--dc22
                                    2009025301

The Dinosaur Next Door

by Joan Stimson

Illustrated by Andy Elkerton

Crabtree Publishing Company

www.crabtreebooks.com

Joan Stimson

"I think dinosaurs are fantastic fun because they come in so many different shapes and sizes."

Andy Elkerton

"I wouldn't like to find a dinosaur in my garden. Think of the mess and all the footprints everywhere. Drawing them is much safer!"

Last night from
my window, this
is what I saw ...

a red and purple
dinosaur —
a dinosaur next door!

The dinosaur ran
around and around.

It gave a great
big roar.

And then it looked
right up at me and
scared me even more.

13

I tried to back away.

But then it shouted,
"Hello Tom! It is party
time. Hooray!"

The dinosaur was
Mr. May, the man
who lives next door.

21

"Enjoy the party,"
I called out. "You are a
super dinosaur!"

22

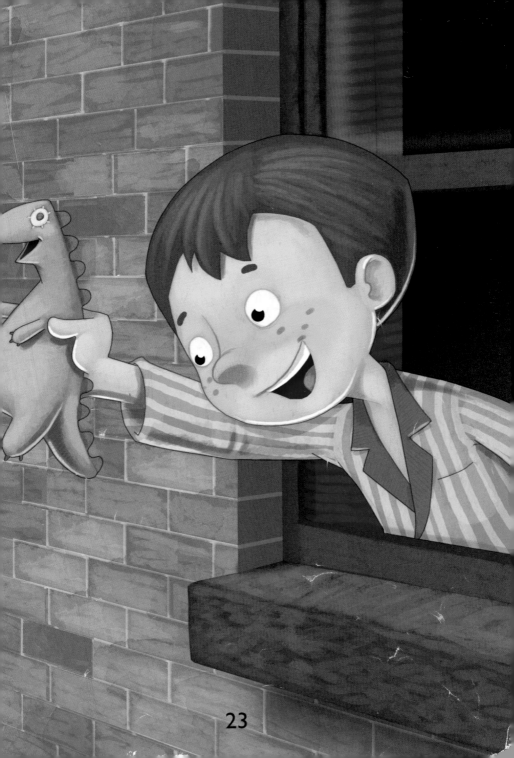

Notes for adults

TADPOLES are structured to provide support for early readers. The stories may also be used by adults for sharing with young children.

Starting to read alone can be daunting. **TADPOLES** help by providing visual support and repeating high frequency words and phrases. These books will both develop confidence and encourage reading and rereading for pleasure.

If you are reading this book with a child, here are a few suggestions:

1. Make reading fun! Choose a time to read when you and the child are relaxed and have time to share the story.
2. Talk about the story before you start reading. Look at the cover and the blurb. What might the story be about? Why might the child like it?
3. Encourage the child to reread the story, and to retell the story in their own words, using the illustrations to remind them what has happened.
4. Discuss the story and see if the child can relate it to their own experiences, or perhaps compare it to another story they know.
5. Give praise! Children learn best in a positive environment.

If you enjoyed this book, why not try another TADPOLES story?

At the End of the Garden
9780778738503 RLB
9780778738817 PB

Bad Luck, Lucy!
9780778738510 RLB
9780778738824 PB

Ben and the Big Balloon
9780778738602 RLB
9780778738916 PB

Crabby Gabby
9780778738527 RLB
9780778738831 PB

Dad's Cake
9780778738657 RLB
9780778738961 PB

Dad's Van
9780778738664 RLB
9780778738978 PB

The Dinosaur Next Door
9780778738732 RLB
9780778739043 PB

Five Teddy Bears
9780778738534 RLB
9780778738848 PB

I'm Taller Than You!
9780778738541 RLB
9780778738855 PB

Leo's New Pet
9780778738558 RLB
9780778738862 PB

Little Troll
9780778738565 RLB
9780778738879 PB

Mop Top
9780778738572 RLB
9780778738886 PB

My Auntie Susan
9780778738589 RLB
9780778738893 PB

My Big, New Bed
9780778738596 RLB
9780778738909 PB

Night, Night
9780778738671 RLB
9780778738985 PB

Over the Moon!
9780778738688 RLB
9780778738992 PB

Pirate Pete
9780778738619 RLB
9780778738923 PB

Rooster's Alarm
9780778738749 RLB
9780778739050 PB

Runny Honey
9780778738626 RLB
9780778738930 PB

The Sad Princess
9780778738725 RLB
9780778739036 PB

Sammy's Secret
9780778738633 RLB
9780778738947 PB

Sam's Sunflower
9780778738640 RLB
9780778738954 PB

Tag!
9780778738695 RLB
9780778739005 PB

Ted's Party Bus
9780778738701 RLB
9780778739012 PB

Tortoise Races Home
9780778738718 RLB
9780778739029 PB

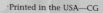

So it was that Cu Chulainn got his name.

Soon he became the best guard in all Ireland.

When the Red Branch Knights saw how good a guard he was, they asked him to join them.

Before long, Cu Chulainn was the most famous Red Branch Knight there ever was.

The ball flew through the air. It struck the hound on the head and killed it instantly.

When Chulainn heard the savage roars, he came rushing out from his castle.

"What have you done to my hound?" he asked Setanta. "Who will now guard my castle against invaders?"

"I will," replied Setanta. "From now on, I will be called Cu Chulainn."

Cu is the Irish word for hound. Cu Chulainn means The Hound of Chulainn.

From the forest came a fierce and savage sound. It was the howl of the Hound of Chulainn, the most feared animal in all Ireland.

The Hound of Chulainn guarded Chulainn's fort against invaders.

Suddenly, the Hound of Chulainn came rushing at Setanta. It was barking and growling savagely.

Setanta was not afraid. He took his silver ball from his pocket and hit it with his hurling stick.

He wanted to meet the Red Branch Knights who would be at the hunting feast.

Once more, he travelled through dangerous forests. Once more, he beat off the wild animals who came to attack him.

When he reached the Fort of Chulainn, Setanta was very tired. He sat down on a rock by the side of the road.

After that, King Connor left and went hunting.

Later that evening, the king would be at a hunting feast. Many warriors from the Red Branch Knights would also be there.

The hunting feast would be at the Fort of Chulainn. The Fort of Chulainn was a big castle that was owned by a local chieftain called Chulainn.

After the king had gone, Setanta set off for the Fort of Chulainn.

A gain Setanta got the better of them all. He knocked them to the ground and broke their sticks.

King Connor Mac Nessa was watching nearby. He was amazed to see his best young warriors beaten by one so young.

"Who are you?" asked the King.

"I am Setanta," replied the young hero. "I have come to join the Red Branch Knights."

King Connor laughed and told Setanta he was much too young.

He ran onto the playing field with his hurling stick in his hand.

Very quickly he had the ball on the end of his hurling stick. He beat every other player on the field and scored a goal.

The young men of the Senior Machrad were angry. They did not like being beaten by one so young.

The whole group set about attacking Setanta.

Amhan Macha was the palace of King Connor Mac Nessa.

Outside the palace, many young men were playing at games and sporting contests. They were members of the Senior Machrad. They were competing to see who could join the Red Branch Knights. They were all much older than Setanta.

On one of the playing fields, a group of young men were playing hurling.

Setanta was very tired after his long journey. Still, he wanted to join in the game.

The journey was long and hard. There were many terrible dangers.

Wolves and wild boars roamed in the forest. There were many more wild animals who would gobble up a young boy.

Each day, Setanta had to fight the wild animals with his spear and his hurling stick.

At night he slept with one eye open.

After many days travelling, he reached Amhan Macha.

When they were much older, only the very best Machrad warriors were allowed to join the Red Branch Knights.

Setanta could not wait that long. One night he crept out of bed and set off to join the Red Branch Knights.

He took with him his spear, his shield and his hurling stick.

He also took with him a special silver ball that his father had given to him as a present.

The Red Branch Knights were the bravest soldiers in Ireland.

Setanta loved hearing stories about the Red Branch Knights.

There and then, he wanted to go off and join them.

"You're too young to join the Red Branch Knights," his father said. "Next year you can join the Machrad."

The Machrad were like Boy Scouts. Young boys who joined the Machrad learned many skills. They learned about hunting and sporting contests. They trained to be young warriors.

When Cu Chulainn was a young boy, he was called Setanta.

Setanta was the son of a very brave warrior, and he wanted to be a brave warrior too.

His father taught him many things. He taught him to hunt and to fish. He taught him to run as fast as the wind. He taught him to be skilled with the sword and with the spear. He taught him many games.

Above all, he taught Setanta to hurl a ball farther and faster than the eye could see.

He also told Setanta many stories. He told him about the Red Branch Knights.

IRISH LEGENDS

Cu Chulainn

Retold by Reg Keating
Illustrated by Heather McKay

Tarantula Books

Published by Geddes & Grosset Ltd,
New Lanark, Scotland, for Owl Records Ltd,
Dublin, Ireland.

ISBN 1 85534 760 1

Printed and bound in the UK

10 9 8 7 6 5 4 3 2 1

D1445065